'The Black Lovers'
Lovers'
and Other Stories

Anna Parijskaia

ISBN: 978-0993218347

CONTENTS

Me

Perhaps my life is like a butterfly swimming, gulping in the reality and diving into a fantasy. I remember the kitchen on the top floor of a Soviet block. I am five and my grandmother is force-feeding me. There is a window behind her with a landscape. It is not a real landscape. It is dramatically shaped clouds coloured by the sunset creating the most beautiful pink lake with little islands surrounded by purple mountains framed by the window right behind her, so I dive in. Swallowing my grandmother's potions was the ransom I paid for the freedom to go out through the door to the courtyard. But my brain is already possessed by the picture I saw in the window, and I begin to spread the idea among the kids that they should leave this world and come with me to see the wonderful pink lakes with purple mountains, and they do.

St Petersburg

In 1992 St Petersburg International Airport hardly existed. The city had only just reclaimed its original name, and was at the beginning of its international fame. Russia, like a sleeping beauty, was waiting to be woken up to a fairy-tale wedding with the West. The dowry and the novelty promised a happy marriage, but it soon turned into a cold winter.

The air is thick like vodka from the freezer; breathing in the cold liquid hurts your lungs. The morning emphasises the blue and dissolves the yellow from last night. People in their heavy coats, like butterflies locked in their cocoons, tread through the snow in slow motion, passing the shimmering patterns of tropical gardens created by frost on the windows, and dream.

We were driving along Moskovsky Prospect, passing the enormous statue of Lenin pointing his arm towards the bright future, but a 1950s Soviet Baroque building blocked the view, so instead he was pointing straight into the bedroom window where the 20-year-old young woman sitting next to me in the taxi was conceived. Who knows how many consummations have been inspired by this statue in the last twenty years. But now it was me pointing for my daughter at his grotesque figure that looked more like a cossack dancer in a winter coat with a hat of snow on top of his gigantic granite head.

On the Nevsky Prospect I could hear the roar of Tsar Godunov on the stage of the Mariinsky Theatre. St Petersburg at night is a snow globe shaken up by memories.

The Black and White Lovers

Curls of fire caged in glass
Tactile Anna on tip toes
Sipping brandy, brows like minks
Slipping off from porcelain
Noble nostrils, royal chin.

She got it from her mamma! The thread of DNA from the black and white lovers in the old photo. Jason is going to be ninety this year and Medea, beside him in the black and white picture, is still beautiful.

Unravelling the thread through generations, Daisy married Needle Steel. He was slick and shiny, strong as needles are. Never bends, and pricks really painfully, leaving ruby dots of blood around her neck for the anniversary. Daisy tried to put the thread through the needle's eye but he had different plans for his exotic-looking bride. A butterfly pricked through, its body pinned onto a purple velvet cushion and preserved in a box as Needle's trophy.

Maria Josephine had a difficult labour and now looked at the baby with tears of joy. At last she had given her husband some pride. She was observant and believed in values. She even shared a joke with other, not so lucky mothers, that her little Needle even poops symmetrically, in little cubes, and the midwife said at the age of twenty-three he will become Needle Steel, a man of Law and Order.

He loved New York. He felt the city was inspired by the story of Creation from the book of Genesis. From the age of six he was forced to read it by his father. He was his father's favourite, and unlike the others, Needle had never let him down. Manhattan's stalagmite skyscrapers are as high as his own desire for success. He felt enraptured in this glib and clean symmetrically erected crystal jungle before he got stung by a bumblebee resting on Daisy's shoulder and suddenly became dizzy. He saw a kaleidoscope of multiple reflections of her delicate beauty in the bright glass maze of the New York City. For the first time in his life Needle realised he was not indifferent to nature. Daisy held some sort of incredible connection with it, something he didn't have, so he asked her to marry him.

He called her Mowgli. Scorpions and bumblebees were her pets. She had resistance to their poison, an amazing gift from nature, a mutation after a snake bite at the age of three. No one believed she would survive, but she did. Medea stayed up all night. She didn't cry. She didn't even pray. She remained still for forty-six hours, and then Daisy opened her eyes. There is healing in stillness.

That quality fascinated Needle to the point that he used every occasion to give her rare and unusual species. He became quite famous among colleagues and clients for his interest in poisonous insects and reptiles. He even entertained his guests showing off his wife's unusual talent. By that time they had moved into a 19th century flat with very high ceilings and crystal chandeliers right next to the Imperial Palace.

Twenty years later she bought a dolls' house from an antique shop in London and it brought to her mind a flash from the past: the Nevsky Prospect all freshly powdered by snow and decorated with a monogram of lights like the stage of the Mariinsky Theatre. Lighted palaces disappeared in the blizzard inside the snow globe, and slowly from her visual memory, leaving only the Schubert tune learnt by little Sasha, which evolved into Rachmaninov in London, and still echoes in Chicago.

Black and white lovers on the photo: Medea sipping something refreshing from a glass, and Jason looking inwards and at peace. She hadn't seen them for a long time. She was on her own lonely journey, away from home, looking for something, but there is only one Golden Fleece and it is meant to be found by Jason. He is going to be ninety this year, and Medea is sitting next to him, still beautiful.

The Box

He'd been a lacquer box inlaid with turtle shell in copper. He looked like it was made by the master-craftsman André Charles Boulle. Some bits were missing but the general feeling was of something grandiose. It was quite mind-blowing suddenly to become a possessor of this rare thing, and it felt so overwhelming to keep and care for it. I chose a place for him that was quite safe but where I could see him from any part of the room at any time. It was such a joy to introduce it to my friends. I could not take my eyes off my box. Even when his body was entangled with mine, my eyes would still be glued to the shelf were it stands, anticipating my desire to discover its contents.

I started gently taking it off the shelf and studying it, looking at every detail, getting to know all the imperfections, scabs, scratches, chips. Some bits were missing from the ornamentation, but on the whole it was exquisite and dear and precious, even though it wasn't new. The more I looked the more I became fascinatedly curious about its contents, but it was locked. It didn't matter at all at first: you have the box, so you have whatever the box contains. One day I made my first attempt to open it. Overwhelmed with excitement I took the box and gently tried the key, but it wouldn't turn. I tried again, with a little more effort, but no, it didn't give. In surprise and disbelief, I decided to be patient and give it some thought. But days passed, and weeks, and years, and increasingly looking at it was not enough – I wanted to see inside. Frustration turned into obsession. I became determined. I tried a screwdriver, a knife, scissors. I broke my teeth on it, but still it wouldn't give. I hammered him again and again. All my friends and neighbours tried to save me but it was too late. I squashed all the decoration and cracked open the box... only to discover it was solid wood with no inside. It was too much for him to bear so he left.

The Skinny Jeans

A few years ago Elaine got confused. In the comfort of her marital home, she got a taste of sex and lust. It happened on one of those party nights when people lose track of the alcohol units, the body begins to relax, and the internal voices disappear, together with the boundaries, and a Pandora's box of the unconsciousness reveals suppressed desires. At the peak of the party, as she went to the cellar to fetch a few more bottles, she suddenly heard shuffling noises downstairs, and caught sight of Ken pulling down a very tight pair of jeans from a very skinny pair of legs. The legs noticed Elaine and did a runner, pushing her out of the way and into Ken's clutches. After a few seconds of wrestling and thirty years of fidelity, Elaine was molested, conquered and seduced in the wine cellar lit by a single dim bulb, to the tremor of a very rare collection of Mediterranean wines, breaking six precious bottles.

The next morning Vince went down to fetch some butter. Still in his pyjamas and bare feet, he stepped on the broken bottles and spilled blood on the crime sin committed by Elaine and her impromptu lover.

The very same morning Elaine woke up with mixed feelings of shame and satisfaction. She suddenly felt energised and decided to hoover the house. Her body was aching, a pleasant reminder of the previous night. Usually these kind of memories evaporate next morning with the fumes of alcohol. Who cares? People do get cared away at parties sometimes. But for Elaine it wasn't just a casual shag. It was a romantic twist in her life which happened once and she wasn't prepared to let it go.

Yes, she committed the adultery, but only because she'd suffered years of loneliness and isolation.

On this bloody morning Ken struggled to open his eyes, but when he did, the first thing he saw was a pair of jeans on the floor and a skinny leg sticking out from under the duvet. He knew instantly it wasn't his own leg; the toes had red vanish on them. He got a bad feeling in his stomach. Yes he overdid it last night, but now he felt repentant. The hangover felt like a crown of thorns on his head, he even touched it to make sure it was an illusion. He also wished that Elaine in the cellar had been an illusion too, but reality hit him in the face like a wet cloth from the dirty laundry. He even stopped breathing for a few seconds.

– Shit!

The problem was that Elaine was his sister-in-law, and Vince was her husband. However, when Elaine heard Vince's scream from the cellar her heart dropped. She realised how badly she had hurt him! She felt deeply for poor old Vince. But her feeling for Ken was much more exciting.

Ken dimly remembered the details of the previous night and he knew he owed her an explanation.

Trying to get out of the cellar, Vince stepped on hiw wounded foot. Sharp pain sliced through his body and he screamed again. It felt like a piece of glass had got stuck in his wound. Elaine was ready to confront him. She was longing for happiness, but Vince seemed to do all the wrong things.

Ken empathized with the couple struggling along the marriage path, so perhaps he could present it, if he had to, as just an attempt to spice up a dying relationship.

Vince was screaming and calling for Elaine to come downstairs. Eventually she was ready to confront him. As she stepped in to the cellar she saw Vince standing in the broken glass in a puddle of red wine mixed with blood. Her heart tightened. She burst into tears and told him all about lust night in the cellar. The pain from his wounded foot helped Vince to bear the pain of his wife's adultery. To tidy up the mess they called in the cleaner. She arrived on time in tight jeans emphasizing a very skinny pair of legs.

Ken was no longer received, ever. Vince's foot slowly healed.

And they all lived happily ever after.

Tarragona

It was stormy for two days and the waves were enormous. When they break into a froth of oxygen bubbles and the bubbles break on your skin, you feel like a strawberry in champagne.

The waves were growing big, like a gigantic glassmaker was blowing them from the bottom of the sea. They looked like molten glass, swollen and round. As they get closer to the shore, growing bigger and bigger, the sun hits them and everything inside the wave becomes transparent. Ginormous tuna fish caught in the wave sparkle for a second before the wave hits the shore and the fish disappear in the glitter of the sand.

Apparently the most sensual organ of the body is the skin. It becomes alive in the warm waters of the sea. The sea bathes every cell, equally caressing every square inch of your body, and under the moonlight, the velvet cover of the Spanish night gently embraces you.

The feasts of Mediterranean seafood haven't changed since Roman times. The restaurants are heaving and the mountains of shells from the feast will be discovered in a thousand years by future generations. That will be all they know about this wonderful night. The meaning, the feeling, will be gone with us. Just as we consume the molluscs, time will consume every single one of us. The feelings and emotions will all be gone. Only the mountains of shells will be left on the Tarragona shore.

The Loss of a Husband

Aline is a plump lady with an interesting tail, but because she is plump she could not see her tail. In fact, she had no idea she had it. Obviously every-body else did, but they didn't know she didn't know, so as a result there was a lot of confusion in Aline's life. Her tail had an independent life, which meant she had no control over it. When Aline saw food or got exited, the tail would fluff up, and would start making seductive, shaky moves. But when nothing interesting was going on in Aline's life, it would get bored, and would swing around Aline's hips, so that she started to suspect some-thing strange was going on behind her back. Then she would call friends to share her worries, and that would be hard for her friends to bear. English people don't tell embarrassing truths, so she remained in ignorance.

Aline lived on the top floor of a tall Victorian building with a beautiful view. She lived alone, as she had lost her husband. That tragic and mysterious event happened on a grey day in January. Aline and her husband were choosing a grey carpet for their living room at John Lewis's. They got lost among the rich choice of grey shades which this respectable British institution provided for its customers. While comparing the shades, he got sucked in by a powerful vacuum cleaner. When Aline noticed, it was too late. She found his glasses on the subtle, grey-coloured carpet just next to the Hoover that had sucked him in. So she bought the carpet as a tribute to her lost husband.

The surreal circumstances of his disappearance left Aline isolated behind a wall of disbelief. Never mind her arrest by the police on suspicion of his murder: the case hit the papers and the news. Everybody was trying to guess whether she was really a murderer, a fantasist or a schizophrenic. In the end she couldn't tell the difference herself, and at that point people started to notice her tail. At her local café, when she squeezed between the tables to grab a free seat, her tail would knock off people's drinks, and that would create such a mess and hassle of clearing up and apologising that it only encouraged the tail to infuriate the customers even more by dipping its tip into people's mugs of coffee. To end the kerfuffle, the manager would offer Aline any coffee she wanted on the house to take away. She appreciated the attention and generosity, but with mixed feelings.

Sometimes, when waiting for a bus, Aline's mind would take a wrong di-rection and start replaying the events of that ill-fated day at John Lewis's. Then the bored tail would start stroking other people at the bus stop. Most people would move off to a safe distance, but some individuals enjoyed this strange experience, and stayed close to Aline.

But the worst was at dinner parties. When sitting next to a male guest, her tail would curl up comfortably on his lap under the table while Aline was engaged in a lively conversation with her neighbour, who was left speech-less. She would put this reaction down to her personality, and with an elegant gesture she would pass him a discreetly perfumed scrap of paper with her phone number scribbled on it.

But he would never call.

Eventually she'd had enough.

One morning, still in bed with a cup of coffee, she was surfing the globe on her computer. On the screen she recognised a picture: the sea, the sun, the sand. It was exactly the scene her therapist had asked her to imagine when he was getting her to relax. And that impelled Aline to reach out for this haven of peace.

She took out her card and typed in the number. A few seconds later it was confirmed. She did not need to imagine the picture in the therapy room any more. The place was real and she was going to fly in.

At last, after months of British gloom, she saw the sun above the clouds. On her arrival, warm air embraced her. She breathed in the tropical fragrance and made her way to passport control. The immigration officer asked the usual questions and stamped her passport, but when she stepped out she was stopped by security and asked about the tail, which didn't match any nationality description. That was the first time Aline came to know about the tail. She was refused an entry visa and was sent back home on the same plane on the same day.

On her return she made an appointment with her therapist. As Aline stepped into the therapy room the dam burst. It seems she had absorbed the moisture of the heavens while she was travelling in the air, and now flooded the therapy room with tears. With feet wet from the flood, the therapist tried to send out empathetic vibes.

"How is it possible after so many sessions and a fortune spent I had no idea about the tail?" Aline cried.

The therapist explained that, within the established boundaries of his profession, it is only possible to discuss what the client brings to a session, and since Aline had never mentioned the tail, it had never been discussed. Besides, Aline should not let the tail undermine the good work they'd done over the years. He reminded her that the opinions of others are merely a projection of their own insecurities. By that time Aline felt like throwing her glass of water at him, but the session was over and she had to leave.

She blamed the Hoover.

So she wrote a letter to John Lewis and demanded an explanation. The reply said:

Dear Aline:

We are very sorry for your loss and the distress it has caused you. We would like to reassure you that the vacuum cleaner involved in the incident was removed by the police from the showroom and sent off for investigation. The results of the investigation have shown no indication of culpability by the vacuum cleaner, as it is incapable of sucking in large objects such as a husband.

As you are a valued customer, however, we would like to offer you some compensation.

We therefor enclose £300-worth of vouchers as a goodwill gesture.

With best wishes,

John Lewis

Aline's health was deteriorating rapidly. She started hearing voices and tried to ignore them, but soon she started receiving text messages from one of the voices that had been talking to her. That in itself would have freaked her out, but the message was simple, short and reassuring.

One morning she woke up in her room. The sun was up, the room was bright, and she let go of her long-disturbed mind. Lying in bed with a cup of coffee, Aline started thinking about the voice that had been talking to her for the last couple of months, and out of control her mind drew a picture of a very handsome man, well build, well mannered, interesting, and in love with Aline. She experienced a pleasant wave of joy, so she gave him the name Jonathan and a job as a lecturer in classical literature. Then she imagined the scent of his cologne, just like his voice: deep, velvety, with a little musky touch. Her internal engine suddenly filled up with water, oil and petrol, the key was turned, and coughing noises started to come out, showing it was still alive.

Aline finished her coffee, got out of bed and looked in the mirror. She looked one size smaller and one inch taller. Her eyes were bright and her tail was gone.

She wanted to call her therapist and tell him about it, but suddenly she was interrupted by an unexpected and very insistent ring on her doorbell.

Separation

I am a very friendly person, but when my ex describes to me my new and bright future he ignites so much rage that I never knew I could contain it. And he does it in a very decent manner, saying, "This is the beginning of a new life."

Which means he's dumping me for my own good.

We were married for 20 years and we know lots of people many of whom are separated. So I asked him to name me just one middle-aged women who has started this incredibly happy new life.

After six months he came up with the answer: "Polly."

"Who the fuck is Polly?"

"My new girlfriend. She's only a few years younger than you. So don't give up, keep looking."

Dear Polly, let me tell you something:

When a man is attentively listening to you he is more mesmerised by the movement of your mouth than by the content coming out of it. That may create the effect of an empathetic listener, and obviously any woman will fall for that. You could end up having a passionate affair or a long-lasting marriage with the guy, but that's beside the point. The point is that after some time that effect will fade away and from the compassionate listener he suddenly turns into a dummy. The biggest mistake of every female is to explain things again and again. The second is to raise the sound of her voice. But he still doesn't get it because he never did. He will start to feel anxious and under attack for no reason. Eventually he will call you obnoxious and run off to a new and more inspiring mouth movement.

I was exhausting myself for so many years trying to make my miserable husband happy, and only now do I see that I was the reason for his misery.

My very darling, eccentric, north London, vegetarian, organic, alternative medicine, ecologically living psychotherapist friend Mina said:

"He is superficial."

Well, maybe, but who gives? At the end of the day he's having his unhealthy English dinner like he always did, but with a new and healthy appetite like he never had.

And suddenly I felt like an orphan panda which had grown up in captivity, now released into the wild to fend for myself.

From My Daughter's Diary

Uncle Toby had never left his cradle. On the day I was born he converted an old Victorian family house into a fortress on top of our flat, and we never saw him again.

My parents met far away at the time when the iron walls and curtains were falling. They met in a grubby kitchen in the most beautiful city in the world, and for six weeks the sun didn't leave the sky. Two years later I was born. I was dropped from my mother's womb into my father's arm, and that was the biggest moment of his life, as he said.

In our flat under Toby's castle we were visited by Laura. Nobody knew exactly who Laura was but when she came the sound of tinkling bells would follow her around, so I think she was a fairy. My dad didn't believe in magic nor in the golden glitter she would scatter on us, but we always needed the money. When she died Uncle Toby wept a lot, so I think she must have been his mother.

I loved Laura. She used to take me to visit her old friend Tom who lived under the roots of an old tree next to Kentish Town station. I loved to play and explore the dark corners of Tom's home. It was full of abandoned things from the High Street, all swept down by the wind or by the dustmen or by streams of rainwater, straight into Tom's cave. There was so much stuff in there: strange, old, useless, long forgotten by the people endlessly shopping on the streets above Tom's cave.

My mother, a giant squirrel, was very worried about the weight above. She was running up and down the walls brushing off the dust from the crashing ceiling with her enormous fluffy tail. My dad, a magnificent elk, could not take the pressure. Like any elk he would be scared away by the tiniest little noise into his study. That's what we all thought, but behind the doors he was hiding from us his real world: the wilderness and the cold air of a great forest. He would wander around there for hours and hours indulging in solitude and silence, feeding on the magic mushrooms and the moss. My mother always wondered how so much mud came out of his study.

After Laura died the flat became scarily silent. Very often I would be woken up in the middle of the night by a subtle sound of tinkling bells, hoping she was walking down the corridor, but realizing it was only a dream. My father never returned from his forest, and mother said that it wasn't my fault: there's just something seriously wrong with the structure of the house.

Psychotherapy

Every time I came to see him I would have to come up the stairs. The first time, I thought he looked like Picasso. His pitch-black eyes have a drilling look as they stare down at me from the top of the stairs, but a smile transforms those black eyes into blue and it's Holger. In the room, in his chair, he looks like a tree twisted by the winds. I want him to like me, so I always try to seduce him with my intellectual paragliding above the clouds in the blue sky filled with glittery golden sunny spells, showing off and inviting him to join me, but he remains there on the ground in his chair, where he's been for the last three hundred years, listening to me. It would last for an hour but stays for eternity.

Dating

Every women has a friend's husband who always gives a slightly more than friendly hug good-bye after a dinner party. His forever faintly sad expression is of a person who hasn't experienced love for a long time, and has been forgotten and pushed out to the edge of family life by his offspring. This is the man to go to in the moment of weakness and despair of abandonment, when you are reaching out for a sole mate who feels the same. But don't get carried away, because the misery of his marriage that he was sharing with you in fact is a happy misery. Yes, they've been happily miserable for thirty-eight years, and still going strong.

So my next decision was to go on a dating site. I just registered for a month to see what my options would be on the free market. I started receiving massages three and a half minutes after I registered. The range of men was from thirty to sixty-five. The sixty-fives turned out to be ten years older – they have so enjoyed the last ten years here that they forgot time flies and they have to change their picture. Some of them have passed away but continue to live on in this dating universe for ever. Sometimes I thought the thirty-year-old man who contacted me must have confused the dating site for an adoption agency, but the confusion was mine; they were very clear about what they are looking for. The computer screen scrolls up and down endless anonymous faces both young and old, all desperately intimidating.

At the end of the month I panicked in desperation to get out of those murky waters, where fat old carp flirt in the depths, only coming to life on the arrival of a new drowned soul. Then they fight for attention to feed their ever-hungry egos, before they sink back into the gloomy depths until their next feed. And if you don't get out in time, the system will start recycling you over and over again.

Colin

Colin was a whale but he didn't know that. He was trying to walk among the people and be like them. He warned me, "I am different." Every time we meet I can see him coming from very far away. It was easy to spot the whale among the people. First he was very big, and second he was moving like a whale, heavy out of water.

I think he missed the ocean a lot. Sometimes when I talk to him about it he gets very sad, because he knows the ocean is too far away and for a whale it would be impossible to get there by land on his own.

I was too small for him in my little boat. He wanted to meet another whale. His slightest move would rock my boat so badly that I was never sure if I would survive or drown. I was drifting further and further away with him, because even in the water he didn't know he was a whale, and seemed so helpless and so unsure and confused. He was calling for other whales.

I would balance in my little boat around him. I could only see one of his eyes at a time. I had to sail all around his face to see the other one. And while I was making this journey from eye to eye he couldn't see me at all, and that meant that for him I didn't exist.

In my little boat I looked like a tear under the whale's eye, a drop in the ocean.

Effi

Effi is a middle-aged man from a warm country. My friend introduced us on Skype. As an experienced dating site user he sent me his picture to attract me. Usually people choose the best one. So did Effi. With a jolly smile and a round belly, Effi was posing on a Land Rover and looking very macho. That was the introduction, and then a phone call on Skype. I didn't answer. I was still living with my ex and it felt strange to chat to a random man, but my dear friend Vera blessed me with permission.

So the next time I heard the loud sound of a Skype video call was at the Maison Blanc café in Muswell Hill. The call was coming from my pocket and attracting a lot of attention. I answered. it was Effi, with his naked hairy chest staring at me from my iPhone. I felt so exposed, and for five minutes I wrestled with naked Effi, and managed to stop him from popping out in the middle of the café only by switching the phone off.

Eventually, after exhausting all the possible Skype stickers of flowers, kisses, hearts and emotions, Effi explained to me that he was only trying to get things going and he wants very much to be pampered and have good sex. Oh who can blame him?

My Daughter

My neighbour Jackie a few years back campaigned against wi-fi. She has an anxiety about radiation, something invisible and dangerous which is after you, perhaps when you are asleep. It's the paradox of a very wealthy neighbourhood: the more you're safe the more you're anxious.

I love my daughter and she is the only one! At the age of eighteen she left me behind with my parental skills and moved out to rent a room in a filthy shared flat in Camden sublet by a drug dealer, with one suitcase and a lot of north London middle-class bullshit, which kept her feeling cramped, but obliged her to keep to the contract. She still hasn't got back her deposit, and ended up paying for her first lesson in real life with half of her student loan.

As a result, she got rid of a lot of useless rubbish from private education, dropped out of uni and became an anarchist. She realized that lapin à la cocotte used to be a fluffy rabbit, and that images of young women are used to feed the greedy mouth of Moloch the modern god of consumerism. She stopped shaving her body and learned how to scare away misogynistic male attention by showing off her armpits, and it worked.

Yesterday she asked about my views on sexual harassment. I was thinking, it would actually be quite nice to be sexually harassed some time, but there is a hope that, like my daughter, I may grow beyond that.

My Father

My father died at ninety-three. He was eager to get to his 90th birthday. He'd lived through every disaster of the twentieth century and survived. He made it to his 90th, and after that he became indifferent, and died at ninety-three in a nursing home. I went to see him after he had a stroke. He recognized me and waved hello. He'd stopped talking. Ninety is long enough to say everything one wants to say and for three years he remained silent. Once in April he was resting in the garden looking at the new blossom on the cherry trees and suddenly he asked, "Have I died?" Two years later he did.

He was born in 1919 in Crimea, Russia, in the middle of the great slaughter of a civil war. Everyone was trying to escape from that hell. So his family joined a small Jewish convoy heading north to safety. A group of horseman stopped the convoy in the middle of the Ukrainian steppe. They asked for money, gold and silver. The frightened people hesitated. Then a horseman grabbed a young woman's first-born child and promised to slice him in half if the Jews didn't pay up. That's how my father was granted his life.

Berlin

Berlin recovered from its wounds. New buildings filled the void and only little memorial plaques with the names of the dead remain to remind us what happened in this cozy and friendly city not so long ago.

Berlin is very easy to understand and quick to get around. It is dominated by a rail track flying over the city, not underground like the London Underground, but above the city in an S-Bahn. Berlin is a simple but also complicated city and contains so many museums, two of which I visited: the Jewish Museum and the National Gallery.

Two different cultures based on two different religions coming from the same roots and existing next to each other for almost a millennium, running parallel through history, crossing over like the rail tracks of Berlin's S-bahn. And sometimes one of the tracks just ends.

Berlin is full of interesting people. You see them sitting at the cafés, the endless kebab shops and oriental restaurants. I met some virtual FB friends for the first time in real life, and the new friends I made in Berlin joined up with me on the universal web of communication.

The S-bahn flew me around and back all day long, and through the windows of the train Berlin was looking up at me all the time.

I always knew I was Jewish but I never knew what it meant. My scary and miserable grandmother spoke Yiddish and I was bullied for it at school, but I left my home town and left the embarrassment behind. Only many years later in another part of the world was I struck again by the tune of my childhood. A sound of prayer, a collective effort to channel a powerful stream of love and devotion, resonated with my soul. it was the sound of a dream that evaporates as soon as you try to hold onto it. Then I started coming to synagogue again and again to listen to the rabbi's voice like I was trying to remember the dream, but it was lost forever.

On Sabbath eve I left Brandenburg Square, filled with young and angry protesters brandishing Syrian flags (history never stops repeating itself), and made my way to the S-bahn. And then the most remarkable encounter happened to me on my way to the synagogue. The train slid into the platform, and the doors opened to reveal a mesmerising sight: the Madonna from Bellini's painting. She was sitting there alive and real, her hair and body covered with white clothing, and a sky-blue scarf under her pale chin matching blue eyes framed by golden eyelashes, and she had a little Jewish boy next to her. Her face shone with such calmness, as if an invisible Angel Gabriel had spread his wings over her. So I followed them.

We made our way to the synagogue together and on the way she told me her story, a story from another Bible, the New Testament: the story of the Madonna and Child. Another parallel and crossing of life and culture and religion. That was Berlin.

Kathy and Mark

Kathy is my friend who lives across the road. She lives with a very wise old cat, Mark, and for many years they raised Kathy's son Tim together. Now Tim is about to get married and soon will become a consultant doctor. Mark is very quiet and fluffy. He purrs a lot and never shows his claws even when Kathy is trying to tease him. Kathy likes to take care of him and makes long journeys to the fishmonger's to get him a nice fish. Because they've lived together for so long, she complains sometimes that Mark never chats to her or cooks for himself (ha! ha! obviously he can't – he's a cat). I find him very comforting and therapeutic, and terribly helpful. When I had my car accident he helped me to fill in the forms. Even Kathy has to admit he's rescued her from Brent Cross shopping mall a few times.

Melissa

Most of all Melissa loved to dress windows. She turned her passion into a profession and talked with a lot of pride about the windows she had dressed. She laughed at people who don't know the truth about windows. The truth is that windows are not "just windows", as some may think, but how to dress them is a philosophy and wisdom and a principle of life, and Melissa may be the first person to have discovered it. A good reason to feel proud, but instead Melissa felt frustration because her discovery was never appreciated.

We met a long time ago, when my very big windows were facing south and didn't have any curtains to restrict the light. Melissa was passing by and the sun reflected from my window for a split second, caught the corner of her eye and invited her in.

Melissa was great fun to be with. She talked to me a lot about the importance of the windows and shared many secrets of how to make them look right, so that they will attract "the right people".

We had so many happy shopping expeditions, when she would point out that some windows are designed for the special people who deserve to be her friends, and some would not pass the face control. Sometimes she would take a window as a personal insult, and to recover, she would invite me for a bite to eat in a nice little restaurant. My life was very bright and happy with my best friend Melissa.

She was very generous with me. Though I have to say, she was very even-handed as well. No one escaped her strict judgement: not a friend, nor even her own sister. I am sure she loved her family but her window principles were never compromised and one day I failed her. My own window, after many years of trust and friendship and shared knowledge, my personal window had cracked. Her fury was devastating. But I survived and am still recovering.

The Messenger

He replied by email: "It sounds like you're having a terrible time and I'm really sorry to hear it. There isn't much I can do from here but I'm due back in London tomorrow morning (Tue 29 Dec 2015) - let me get home, go to the supermarket, have breakfast, maybe sleep a little, and then I'll call you."

His plane took off from Delhi airport to make an overnight flight to London. It was slowly drifting through the night on high altitude and high speed, so peaceful in the clear sky lit by the stars, and the steady sound of the engines sent me off to sleep.
And that felt like the beginning of a new dream.

Angel translates from Hebrew as messenger. So I was dreaming of an angel Jacob flying over from India with the divine message for me, an answer to all my questions, the end to all my confusion, even the end of this story.

Jet-lagged and exhausted with the cold, Jacob hosted me. His home has layers upon layers of the years he's lived there – maybe twenty or thirty layers. Nothing seemed to be removed or revisited. I was sitting in the chair opposite him watching how the smoke from the fireplace mixed with fumes of hashish sending him off from the room back to the high altitude, leaving me alone with no messages.

And again the excruciating pain of letting go false expectations triggered a panic attack. I took my valium and left. The fresh air cleared my lungs.

The number twelve bus picked me up and in forty minutes brought me back to earth, to a festive Oxford Street with Christmas lights, and jolly windows offering 50% discounts.

Heroin

Misha Sands, his mother's first-born daisy baby, golden in the middle and white all round. The joy, the hope, a little angel boy manipulating divine sounds from a giant black lacquer grand piano. The stem of an Iris, tall and handsome, attracted by darkness, bravado and danger. Caught up in the flow with no right to return, sleeping in dust on another continent, grasping life through his mother's umbilical cord, as long as her heart keeps pumping.

The Riddle

The light went off and it was dark. Only screaming voices on the other side begging him to stop. He was holding on tight to the ropes and swinging them faster and faster. His friends and anyone who cared for him would get drawn into this carrousel of screaming people and only the wise kept a safe distance. He didn't notice them, nor the screaming crowd. He remembered another black, warm, weightless, murky gloop, holding onto his own erect penis like a thumb. Hearing the sound of the heavy, steady rhythm of countless carriages shooting through. And then suddenly he felt squeezed, suffocated and pushed out. Bruised, hurt by the sharp light, he was right in the spot of it. Surrounded by the tapestry of faces. All of them talking, coughing and laughing at the same time. Were they laughing at him? Who can say? He'd never seen his own reflection, never seen his own face but he'd been told that he was ugly. His hands were small and soft like dough. When he was dozing in the day he used them as cushions. When he was sitting down he could see his massive square knees, and underneath the knees, the feet with huge big toes.

He remembered the first time he'd left the room. A friend of his father's had taken him for a ride on a motorbike with a sidecar. He still remembered it very vividly. The roaring bike suddenly stopped and he embraced the silence, the sound of the cosmos. The pine trees, like copper columns, reaching out to God, and the microscopic galaxies floating in the golden light sifted through their trunks. He breathed it in, and is still holding his breath.

At the age of five he was only thirty-nine inches away from the ground so he could see all the wildlife in the garden where his father used to take him. Breaking through the jungle of the green stems he got ambushed by a grasshopper suddenly springing out onto his trousers, herds of busy ants carrying stuff in and out, fluffy bumblebees flirting, buzzing morning tunes to every flower, shiny beetles undistracted from their task, hairy caterpillars and their colourful reincarnation, dancing butterflies, and above all this intensity the canopy of flower heads: yellow, orange, pink, red and scarlet, looking up and following the sun. They were already lonely but happy days.

He remembered very few kindnesses but he remembered them all: a beautiful woman put her hand on his head and whispered something sweetly fragrant in his ear; riding on top of his father's shoulders and suddenly empowered by the view from above; his mother's white gown shielding him from nightmares and fever.

There was another woman he met once, very tall and beautiful. She overpowered him with her perfume and he got lost in associations, trying to catch the essence, but she left and her fragrance evaporated into the air as if she had never existed.

He was wondering around deserted streets looking for someone, and was unexpectedly adopted by a black German shepherd. And again the sound of the everlasting train became louder. The golden forest was covered in snow, frozen. In one stroke the passing train knocked off the white burden from the pines and stopped. He left the carriage followed by the dog. Giant seagulls spotted the rare game and spiralled around him weeping like a crowd of grieving widows. They lifted him off the ground and he submitted himself to the dozens of white wings. They would have carried him away but the black German shepherd barked and attacked the spiral. The wings let go and he fell onto the ground. Surrounded by mist, he saw a spot and it was growing, and another, and more. it was the fisherman disciples returning from the mist before dark. They left the mist completely empty. The everlasting train kept on running in his head but his heart was beating even faster. The screaming voices on the other side were begging him to stop. He let go of the ropes, inhaled the mist, embraced the emptiness and started to run faster until he got completely swallowed by the mist and only the lonely black shepherd dog kept on howling, calling for him.

Mina

Mina is so very busy around the house all day long. She puts on her dungarees and pretends to be a white fluffy mother bunny, feeding and looking after endless needy bunnies around her, including her own grown-up children. But there's something in her eyes and the sound of her giggles that makes me very suspicious: is she really what she seems? I think she's one of those flying kind of women, like in The Master and Margarita, with something witchy about her. And sometimes, when she talks about Prince Charming, I can imagine her just leaving all this needy crowd to take off beyond the clouds and engage with him in the most divine orgy, such as mortals never dare. Yes, this kind of love only exists behind the clouds, and it's waiting for Mina, but she isn't ready to take off yet.

New Year

Mina allowed me to dwell for a few nights in her sanctuary to recover from the last severe punches of the departing bastard, the old year. Some Russians have a superstition that we hold the power to manipulate the future by doing something symbolic on the eve. I have learned from previous years to lower my expectations and stop fretting about it, but I agreed to spend New Year's Eve at a club for the first time in twenty years. The city was expecting something to happen but the security looked well prepared, and reassuring. The most desirable kernel of the city was closed to cars and we had to cover it on foot. Dozens and dozens of festive pairs of naked legs were also marching to the new year and new hopes wearing excruciating sexual fantasies on their feet. It isn't easy to walk like that, so why do so many woman keep walking?

At the club I had a coffee martini and I danced a lot, and precisely at midnight among the happy crowd I watched the London Eye burst into little colourful pieces and ripped up 2015 in a spectacular firework display. The crowd raged and screamed with me and I felt it was my glamorous revenge.

I came down to the kitchen and the new grey day was already waiting for me. I felt that the smell of fresh coffee would be a good start for both of us. Then Mina came and we left the sleepy house. But the streets of London were sleepy too. Mina was driving us around looking for an exciting place to eat. Everything to do with Mina is an adventure, even picking up the laundry from the laundrette. Mick even said we were lesbians. Well, that's his projection: he shouldn't make assumptions about people just on the basis that they refuse to have sex with him.

All the trendy places were asleep too, when suddenly Drummond Street came to mind. A tiny oasis of an old London surround by the modern crystal symbols of money and success, it is still there and open and very reliable. We stepped into India. The smell, the music was exotic and appetizing, and for £6.50 we were offered a home-made buffet with an overwhelming variety of starters, mains, chutneys and desserts. And a very handsome Indian Englishman gave me a guided tour through every dish. It was my first taste of the new year and it was delicious.

Thanks to Nina, Daniel, Lisa, David, Louise and Jane and Paul for support and encouragement.

Made in the USA
Charleston, SC
21 June 2016